Are You A bird?

BY: DR. CAMERON ASHLEY GONZALES

This book is dedicated to Trent. He is a delightful little boy who has blessed our lives with his happy loving personality, inquisitive nature, delight for learning new things, and passion for exploring the wonders of books.

This is your mother.
One day your mother built a nest.

Your mother laid eggs in the nest, and you were inside one of the eggs. While you were inside the egg, you grew.

One day you hatched and came out of the egg.

YOU ARE A BIRD!

You were very hungry when you hatched from the egg.
You could not fly off to catch worms.

Do not worry.
Your mother caught worms and chewed them up for you.
She put them in your mouth.

Each day you watched your mother fly away and catch food so you could grow.

As you ate, you grew stronger and grew more and more feathers.

Your wings grew strong and soon you were ready to fly.

After you were strong, you jumped from your nest, flapped your wings as hard as you could, and flew into the sky just like your mother.

When your brother and sister were ready to fly, they flew too.

One day, you will be ready to be a parent.

You will build a nest for your eggs.

Your babies will hatch and grow.
You will catch worms and bring them to
your babies.

The End

Biography of Author

Cameron developed her love for all things creative at a young age. A dancer, musician, and avid reader, she could often be found quietly reading in the corner of the family's motorhome. Raised by two school administrators in Orange Country, California, avid reading was a family trait.

Cameron completed her undergraduate education in music and English on a music scholarship for Jazz at Chapman University. She earned a teaching credential and degrees in Cross Cultural Education, Curriculum and Instruction and specialties in Gifted and Reading Instruction. She has taught elementary, middle and high school students.

A university professor of 15 years, Cameron has provided instruction for new teachers. She earned a Doctor of Education and an Education Specialist degree from Ball State University. Cameron's dissertation research focused on successful principal leadership in high achieving Title I schools.

Over the past 15 years Cameron has lived and worked in Italy, Germany, South Korea, and Cuba and is currently serving military students and families as a Gifted and ESOL Specialist in Cuba with her son, Trent.

Are You a Bird?

Lesson Plan Developed by Dr. Cameron Gonzales

A NEWBORN BIRD FINDS HIS PLACE IN THE ENVIRONMENT AND ANSWERS THE QUESTION, "ARE YOU A BIRD? AS HE GREW, HE LEARNED ABOUT HIS DEVELOPMENT AND HIS ROLE IN THE ENVIRONMENT.

> **ALIGNS TO THE FOLLOWING COMMON CORE STANDARDS FOR K-5**
> (ELA= English Language Arts)
> ELA RE Literature- Standards 1, 2, 3, 4, 5
> ELA Speaking and Listening- Standards 1, 2, 3, 4, 5

OBJECTIVES:

1. TO HELP CHILDREN DEVELOP AN UNDERSTANDING OF THE LIFECYCLE OF A BIRD.
2. STUDENTS KNOW AND UNDERSTAND THE CHARACTERISTICS OF LIVING THINGS, APPRECIATE THE IMPORTANCE OF THE DIVERSITY OF LIFE, AND BEGIN TO RECOGNIZE THE INFINITE NUMBER OF WAYS THAT LIVING THINGS CAN INTERACT WITH EACH OTHER AND WITH THEIR ENVIRONMENT.
3. DESCRIBE THE BASIC NEEDS OF ANIMALS (WATER, FOOD, SHELTER, AND AIR) AND PLANTS (WATER, LIGHT, AIR, AND NUTRIENTS).
4. STUDENTS KNOW AND UNDERSTAND HOW ORGANISMS CHANGE OVER TIME IN TERMS OF BIOLOGICAL EVOLUTION AND GENETICS.

METHOD:

TEACHER OR PARENT WILL FACILITATE A DISCUSSION THAT INCLUDES READING THE BOOK "ARE YOU A BIRD" BY CAMERON GONZALES. THIS WILL GIVE CHILDREN BASIC KNOWLEDGE ABOUT THE LIFE CYCLE OF A BIRD. THE CHILDREN WILL BE INTRODUCED TO KEY CONCEPT VOCABULARY (LIFE CYCLE, HATCH, HATCHING, FLEDGING, NESTLING, JUVENILE, AND LAID) AND SHOWN PICTURES IN THE BOOK TO PROVIDE CONTEXT TO THE VOCABULARY. CHILDREN WILL DISCUSS WITH AN ADULT THE CONCEPT OF LIFE CYCLES AND DISCUSS HOW LIFE CYCLES APPLY TO ALL LIVING ORGANISMS.

IMPLEMENTATION:

Read the book, then facilitate a class/family discussion about life cycles. Have children think of other organisms with life cycles. Ask open-ended questions about why life cycles are important. Guide children to predict why it is important for the bird to find a mate and lay an egg to reproduce.

K-3: Next make a copy of the worksheet pages that follow these directions. With a parents support, have the child cut out the images for life cycle of the bird and work with them to put the pictures in chronological order (to create a timeline). Help the child turn the timeline of events into a cyclical image representing a bird's lifecycle on the large bird picture. Use the completed image on the next page to check the child's work before gluing the images onto the page of the bird. The adult will help the child draw arrows connecting all the images and label the life cycle map. This board will serve as visual to remind them of the cyclical nature of life cycles and serve as a discussion guide for review.

4-5: Look at the images on the worksheet pages. With parent/teacher supervision, go online and select a free pictochart tool. Find images similar to those provided on the worksheet to demonstrate the stages of a bird's development using the academic vocabulary terms **Egg, Hatchling, Nestling, Fledgling, Juvenile, and Adult.** Place the pictures you select for each developmental stage in a circular image to represent the cyclical nature of a life cycle. At the bottom of the pictochart, define each of the terms used to describe the stages of the life cycle of birds in your own words. Have a teacher/parent check the sample pictochart provided. Be creative and design your pictochart to be a poster that can be used to teach friends and family about lifecycles.

MATERIALS:

Book, Poster board, Marker, (optional copy of life cycle images), 4-5 adult supervised use of a computer

CONCEPTS:

Understanding the life cycle of organisms with the ability to use academic vocabulary to define the stages of a bird's development.

CONCLUSION:

Allow children to orally share their life cycle board or PictoChart and tell about the academic vocabulary words and pictures they selected and how they represent the continued life of organisms in an ecosystem. (This could be in a private place in their room, or in a public setting like a school or church bulletin board.)

Bird
Life Cycle

Are You A Bird?

Bird Life Cycle

Egg - are laid by female birds in nests in number ranging in number from just 1-17. They are incubated by one or both parents for a period of time until the embryo inside has developed

Hatchling - has just hatched and may have only a few feathers and with closed eyes, cannot care for itself

Nestling - nestlings are chicks that are a few days old and are covered in soft feathers. They must still be fed by their parents

Fledgling - chicks that have flight feathers and wing muscles, but are still care for by parents

Juvenile - the short time a bird is an awkward teenager

Adult - are mature and are able to reproduce

Made in the USA
Middletown, DE
11 September 2022

73407647R00018